D0472747

BO

DISCARD

eron

elle Olsen

o. Ltd.

Text © Anne Cameron 1988
Illustrations © Nelle Olsen 1988
Cover and Book Design by Gaye Hammond
ISBN 0-920080-63-4

Harbour Publishing Co. Ltd.
Box 219, Madeira Park, B.C.
Canada   V0N 2H0

Canadian Cataloguing in Publication Data

Cameron, Anne, 1938 —
  Lazy boy

    ISBN 0-920080-63-4

    1. Indians of North America—Northwest Coast of North
America—Legends—Juvenile literature. I. Nelle Olsen II.
Title.
PS8555.A43L3 1988   j398.2'089970795
            C88-091123-9

Printed and bound in Canada

10 9 8 7 6 5 4 3 2

When I was growing up on Vancouver Island I met a woman who was a storyteller. She shared many stories with me, and later, gave me permission to share them with others.

This woman's name was KLOPINUM. In English her name means "Keeper of the River of Copper." It is to her this book is dedicated, and it is in the spirit of sharing, which she taught me, these stories are offered to all small children. I hope you will enjoy them as much as I did.

Anne Cameron

One day, a baby boy was found on the beach. An ordinary enough looking baby boy with no distinguishing marks or tattoos on his body.

The people who found him supposed he was the son of fishing people who had been dropped under the waves when their dugout capsized, or maybe even dragged under by a blackfish or a huge halibut.

They knew that Orca, who feeds her own babies with milk from her breasts, as do women, would have heard the little boy crying, and because there is a link between Orca and the milk-drinking children of women, she would have delivered the orphan child to the edge of the water near the village.

Orca has always been a friend to people, but people have not always been friendly towards Orca, nor have we been as considerate of her children as she has been of ours.

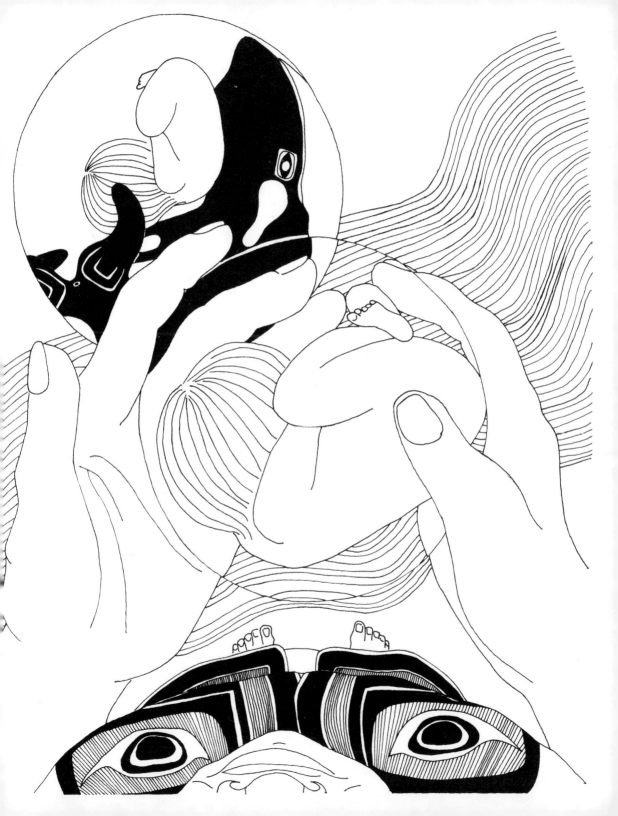

The people dried the salt spray from the chubby body of the orphan baby and fed him small pieces of baked fish, some lily root baked in ashes and chewed soft by the older women, and they gave him sips of nettle-leaf tea, which he sucked from the edge of a small thin bowl. He burped and laughed, waved his baby arms and legs happily, and went to sleep.

He wakened only when he was hungry, and the people fed him willingly, even though years passed and he grew bigger and bigger and hungrier and hungrier and larger and larger until he was twice the size of a grown man.

Four times a day the giant would waken and ask for food, and four times a day the people would feed him, he would smile, thank them, then go back to sleep again.

Everyone called him Lazy Boy and wondered if the day would ever come when he would do some work and begin to justify his existence.

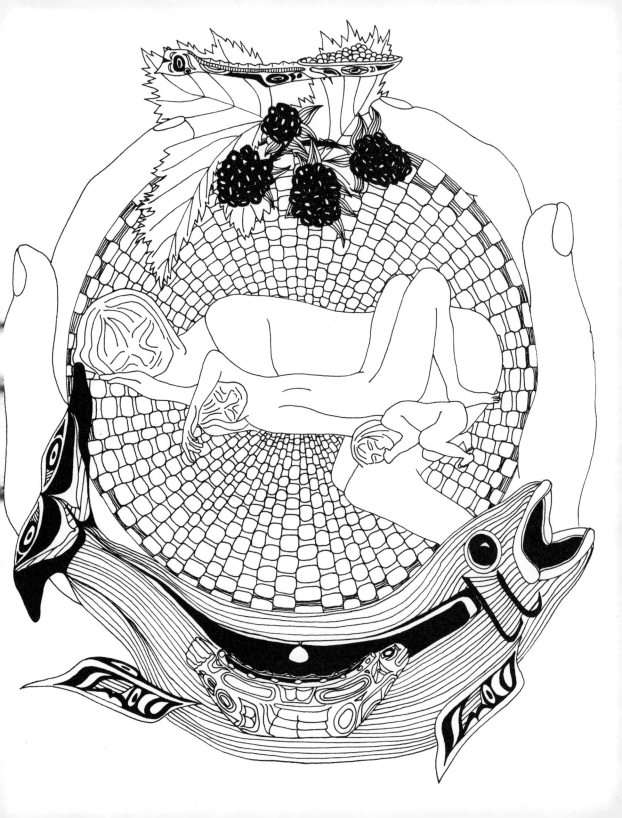

One day Old Man coughed, and the pole holding the world in place trembled. Then the creeks and even the rivers began to overflow their banks, the tide came in and kept on coming, and the lakes moved down to join the sea.

The people gathered the elderly and the infants in their arms and ran for safety, yelling at Lazy Boy to get up, to flee. When he didn't, some of the strong young people ran back and tried to rouse him, but he continued snoring.

They tried to lift him and carry him, but he was too big and too heavy.

"He'll wake up," they assured each other hopefully, "as soon as the water gets in his ears. Nobody can sleep with water in his ears," and they ran to save their own lives.

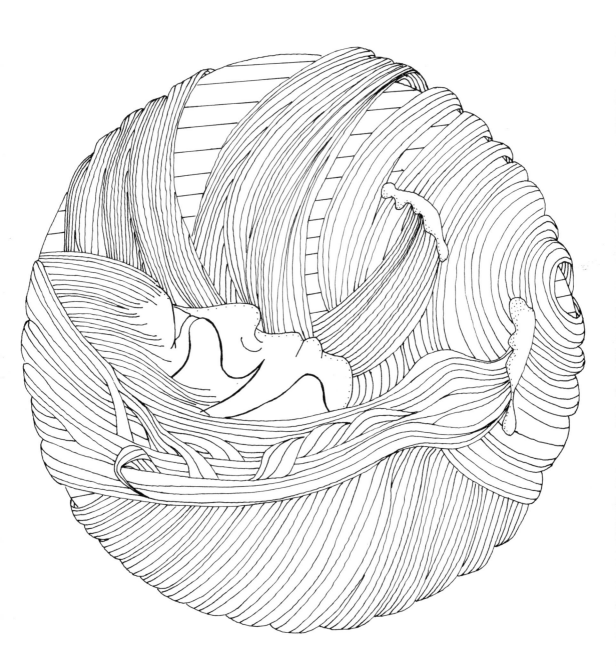

Sure enough, as the water entered his ears, Lazy Boy woke up and realized immediately what had happened. To the total amazement of his foster sisters, foster brothers, and foster parents, he stood up, taller and taller and taller, stretching himself until the clouds surrounded his head like a helmet. He raised his arms, spread his fingers, and from his mouth a sound issued unlike anything heard since Tem Eyos Ki sang her song, and the surface of the water quivered.

He sang again, and the channels of the rivers deepened, the basins of the lakes sank, the water began to recede to fill the holes, leaving fish stranded in the bottom branches of the trees, hanging like fruit, food to replace what the people lost when the smokehouses were flooded.

Then Lazy Boy shrank down to his normal size, which was still huge, and he lay down and went back to sleep.

The people returned to their villages, and four times a day they willingly fed the dozing giant who smiled sleepily and often yawned contentedly, even while accepting the food the people prepared.

Then the trees started growing closer and closer to the village, moving down the hillsides, pushing nearer, threatening to shove the very houses into the chuck, and it was the sound of axes clanging desperately that wakened the huge boy sleeping in the sun.

He watched for a few moments, rubbing his eyes in puzzlement. Everyone who could was fighting the trees, even little children had sharp sticks or bone knives, sawing and slashing frantically at elderberry and fir, cedar and pine, alder and aspen, even at the sacred redclothed arbutus that combines the characteristics of both kinds of trees, having leaves like deciduous, but not losing them all in the fall, staying green through the winter like the conifers.

Lazy Boy rolled himself in a ball, as if he were frightened, then he started to roll around the periphery of the village, uprooting the trees and piling them together neatly, weaving them into a big fence, and when he had cleared even more space than there had been before the trees went berserk, when everything was neat again, he rolled back to his favourite sleeping place and curled comfortably on his side, smiling as he dozed.

The people hadn't yet recovered from their amazement when the most marvelous of all marvels began to happen, a thing so wonderful it is called, simply, The Glory.

A bright light began to glow on the surface of the sea. Flashing like the scales of Sisiutl, the magic sea serpent, bright scarlet, sharp yellow, blue as a dragonfly, green as the outer shell of the June beetle, shimmering and glowing, flashing and sparkling, closer and closer The Glory came until the air began to tremble, and the earth to quiver with the vibrations of the colours.

A young girl who had been unable to hear the sounds of voices put her hands over her eyes and fell to her knees, her head shaking violently as the tremors of colour pounded the bones that grew across her ear canals, powdering them, and she was the first to hear the sound the glowing paddles made as they sliced the sea.

Lazy Boy leaped to his feet and stretched his massive arms towards the glow, tears of joy coursing down his cheeks and landing on the grass, where they turned into tiny strawberries.

The gigantic dugout scraped onto the beach and three very old men dressed in beauty stepped out, the colours flashing on their capes and kilts, and each of these ancients was nearly as tall as Lazy Boy himself.

The people trembled in fear, and only the girl who had once been deaf dared to smile and step forward, hands outstretched in peace, thanking the Supernatural Uncles for their gift to her, the gift of birdsong, the gift of the sound of the wind high in the green trees, the gift so many of us take for granted.

"Thank you," she said, hearing the sound of her own voice for the first time.

"Thank you," Lazy Boy said, with a voice as beautiful as that of Loon before her neck was stretched and her song silenced. "You have protected me in my helplessness and fed me in my hunger. You have kept me warm and given me drink when I thirsted. Without your love, I would have died, and there would have been nobody to replace my fourth uncle when he became too old to continue his work. My fourth uncle is Old Man who holds the world in place at the end of a long pole, and now his brothers have come to take me to him so that I can continue the work and he can retire and enjoy his old age." And the people knew that if they had not cared for the baby Orca had delivered to their beach, this day would have been the day the world ended.

Lazy Boy walked to the dugout, got in, and lifted a golden paddle. His three ancient Supernatural Uncles climbed in with him and the magic craft took off for the other world.

There was a moment when the pole was transferred from the old back to the strong young back, a moment when the earth shifted and the bird of menstrual cramps squeezed through the hole, but Frog Woman taught us the kneeling position to defeat the cramps, so the bird was thwarted.

Sometimes, even today, the earth shifts and trembles. This happens when Lazy Boy hears a joke, and his giggles make his shoulders move.

25

OTHER BOOKS BY ANNE CAMERON

FOR CHILDREN

How Raven Freed the Moon	$4.95 paper
How the Loon Lost Her Voice	$4.95 paper
Orca's Song	$4.95 paper
Raven Returns the Water	$4.95 paper
Spider Woman	$4.95 paper

FOR ADULTS

Earth Witch	$5.95 paper
The Annie Poems	$7.95 paper
Dzelarhons: Myths of the Northwest Coast	$8.95 paper
Stubby Amberchuk & the Holy Grail	$19.95 cloth
Child of Her People	$12.95 paper

Available from Harbour Publishing
Box 219, Madeira Park, BC, V0N 2H0